ESTABLISHING
J.O.Y.

A LEADERSHIP FABLE

Nicole Crews Carter

TABLE OF CONTENTS

ACKNOWLEDGMENTS

The ultimate three-person team, the Father, the Son, and the Holy Spirit deserves all the praise for not allowing me to forget the J.O.Y. vision given to me 10 years ago. In addition, the following faithful family and friends helped cultivate the writing of this book.

Pastor Carter, the love of my life, for being exactly what I need when I need it. Your undying love and support allows me to walk in my God given purpose.

James and Margaret for dragging me to Sunday school and church EVERY Sunday and for making sure that I thought for myself instead of following the crowd.

Courtney and Mikayla for the encouraging look in your eyes that keep me going. It shows how proud you are of me. The two of you have been such a blessing.

My siblings (Delvin, Melonie, and Anthony) for providing me with my first leadership opportunity. As the oldest, you taught me how to think of others before self.

JD for being the big brother that I've needed over the years. You will never know how much that means to me.

Pam L. and Tracy J. for always being there when I need you. The two of you embody true friendship.

Apostle Nicole B. for providing much needed prayers, feedback, and support. Your willingness to help women birth their visions is such a blessing to the body of Christ.

FOREWORD

By Nicole Bonds

Since the beginning of time humans have been tasked with leadership. God gives a mandate to Adam and Eve to be fruitful, multiply, and dominate in the book of Genesis. With this great mandate came opposition from the adversary, Satan, that resulted in the fall of man and the necessity for man to be put back in the place God originally had for them. It would be through Jesus Christ, the savior of the world, that man would have an opportunity to truly gain back their place of authority and power through the sacrificial death, burial, and resurrection of Jesus. I say this to say there is a need even today to be reminded of the power and authority we walk in, the mandate to spread the message and love of God with others, and to live a life pleasing to God.

This book you're reading right now is a modern-day tool carefully written in a manner to help women and men understand the true essence of leadership and the components that allow us to flourish in our unique callings. Although it's fiction, as you read you'll quickly see how real and relevant it is.

If you're wondering why you seem to always be drafted to lead projects or efforts, if you're wondering where to begin to get on the path God has for you, if you need an example of someone who conquered what seemed impossible, if you've made more mistakes than you care to share but still desire to fulfill purpose in your life, and if you need direction on how to begin using what God gave you, this leadership book is for you.

Nicole Carter, is an author, learning enthusiast, a devoted wife and mother, an educator, a champion for women and men of all backgrounds who may be young but desire to live their best life now. Nicole is determined and poised to make an impact on the generations coming after her. She is passionate about seeing others become. I believe in her and what she has been called to do.

I've read this book and connected with a story of survival, overcoming tragedy, isolation, betrayal, resurrection, and elevation that can happen in the life of any of us. As I read this book I was reminded of this scripture,

> *10 After you have suffered for a little while, the God of all grace [who imparts His blessing and favor], who called you to His own eternal glory in Christ, will Himself complete, confirm, strengthen, and establish you [making you what you ought to be]. 11 To Him be dominion (power, authority, sovereignty) forever and ever. Amen.* 1 Peter 5:10-11

As you began to read each chapter, you may recognize that some of their stories may resemble yours. Within these same pages are wisdom lessons, life lessons, and leadership lessons. Prepare to take a journey that will ultimately lead you to a place of established JOY!

INTRODUCTION

She finally received what she had been praying for….. A JOB!!! Priscilla had graduated from college a year ago but had yet to find sustainable employment. Sustainability was critical as she had a one year old who depended on her mom to take care of her. Yes, the one year old who was her college graduation present. In fact, majority of the graduation pictures exemplifies her bundle of joy in her beautiful red dress. Back to the job…Priscilla has always been a hard worker so when she received a degree after 3 ½ years, she just knew finding a job in her field would be a breeze. Unfortunately, it wasn't that easy.

Immediately after graduation (a year ago), she elected to stay in Pittsboro where she attended Grace University. After all, that's where her future husband was still pursuing his business degree. Steve helped her find a great place to stay in the outskirts of the city. He believed it was only fitting that his daughter had the best accommodations. Or that's what he wanted "Cilla", as he so affectionately called her, to believe. So, Priscilla and her beautiful bundle of joy moved to the country (about 15 miles from the city).

Priscilla was fortunate to be able to work full-time for the employer that she worked for part-time during the final months of school. She settled for this position, thinking that experience is much better than a huge pay check. Right?!?!?!? She soon found out that was soooooo far from the truth. You see, milk, pampers, food, gas, rent, and day care expenses added up to be more than what she made even being full-time. There were decisions that must be made. IMMEDIATE Decisions!

The church where her daughter went to day care was having a leadership conference and she was invited as a recent graduate to share her college experience with the youth of the church. At the time of the invitation she had no idea how her life would be impacted. When she went to the conference she found that there were many church leaders from all over the country there to share with others how to be effective leaders. Her curiosity led her to attend a session on JOY. She recalls thinking that was lacking in her life right now. Here she was a recent graduate with a baby, barely making ends meet…. Oh, and her beloved Steve moved her to the country, so she couldn't see what he was doing…. but we will get into those details later.

The session on JOY was beginning in 30 minutes. She rushed her daughter to the free childcare facility for the conference and darted to the room. "Just in time", said one of the conference assistants, "We were about to close this session as it is completely full." She took the last seat in the very back anticipating all the JOY she would leave the session with. Then this husky hairy yet handsome light skinned gentleman took the center of the room as if he was a big-time celebrity. With a roaring voice, he simply said, JOY!

PART ONE – JESUS (the foundation)

CHAPTER ONE

Priscilla is sitting in the large classroom looking around at the approximately 50 people staring at the handsome gentleman anticipating what he is going to say next. Her mind racing at the ways he is going to explain to them how to have JOY. Her first thought was prayer...You know.... that's what all church folk say when you are feeling down. When she found out that she was pregnant, the church folk said, "we'll pray for you". When her daughter was sick, the people at work said, "we'll pray for her". When her aunt died at 35...EVERYONE said, "we'll pray for you and your family". She sat there and thought, he is going to teach us how to pray about every situation to the point that we are always happy. But in that same thought she remembered those individuals that said they would pray during those times......They didn't seem happy. In fact, they most often had a frown on their face and don't let something go wrong with them.... they would cuss in a minute. So maybe he isn't going to talk about prayer.

Perhaps he is going to give us another bible story about how God parted the Red Sea for Moses, or how the Fish ate Jonah, or Noah building the Arc, or maybe Jesus turning water into wine or feeding the 5000. Priscilla thought to herself.... *"I went to Sunday School every Sunday when I was growing up......I know all about the stories. I'm not sure how much JOY we will get out of the*

3

stories. They were great conversation pieces in Mother Liz's junior class, but not here with all these grown folks."

Then almost instantly, she thought about spiritual hymns. She recalled how her mom and grandmothers would sing hymns while they were cleaning the house. They would often say that they didn't like cleaning; however, you could never tell. Granny would sing with such enthusiasm and it seemed like she thoroughly enjoyed swiping every dust particle, sweeping all the trash, and caressing each of the thousands of little trinkets she dusted. All the while calling on the name of the Lord to Pass Her Not, proclaiming that it was Nothing But the Blood, and Priscilla's personal favorite…. her granny encouraging herself to Hold to God's Unchanging Hand. Yes, that must be what he will be talking about today. He will explain how the hymns that brought our ancestors through slavery will give us JOY.

As Priscilla was visualizing her granny singing those songs while washing dishes and what seemed like forever … Bishop Justice once again bellowed out the word JOY. He then immediately proclaimed that the JOY he speaks of is an acronym. The acronym stands for J – Jesus, O – Others, and Y – You. He then showed a slide that illustrated three shapes and said, "now you see it now you don't". As quickly as he showed the shapes, he went to the next slide.

He passed out slips of paper and asked us to write down in our own words our first impression or thoughts about each of the shapes shown on the board. "You only have 2 minutes so write fast."

Priscilla's mind began to twirl as if it were an EF3 tornado. What in the world were the shapes? He put them up and took them down so fast. But to be obedient she began scribbling. There were about 4 rectangles, maybe a few triangles and a square or two. After what seemed like 30 seconds, Bishop said time was up.

At that moment, he brought back to the screen the picture of the third shape and asked that we look at it closely. Bishop instructed us to now write down what we think the shape is or what it represents. This time we only had 1 minute.

Priscilla thought for a few seconds, then she wrote on her paper …. an upside-down table. She said to herself confidently, this is a table that was turned upside down. Oh yes, we are getting ready to discuss what makes Jesus angry. She recalled her high school Sunday School class, led by Rev. Hall. Rev. Hall shared with the class Jesus turning over the tables when they were gambling in the church. Bishop Justice is going to share with us that true JOY comes when we please God. She thought to herself further…."I believe I've got this session figured out." Priscilla pulled out her bible and flipped to the first book of the New Testament – Mathew and went to the 21st chapter. She said to herself. "Yep there it is….the den of thieves/robbers".

"He overturned the tables of the money changers and the benches of those selling doves. 'It is written,' he said to them, "My house will be called a house of prayer, but you are making it a den of robbers."' – Matthew 21:12-13 NIV

Just as she finished that thought, Bishop Justice pulled up the next picture and asked that they do the same thing. Write down what comes to your mind when you see the picture.

Now this picture was a little bit more challenging. Initially, Priscilla thought that it was a house, but it was not proportionate. The roof was bigger than the house itself. So, she then thought that it was simply a triangular block placed on top of a rectangular block. But what does that have to do with JOY? Well this will have to be one that she doesn't get right. Let's move on to the third picture, she thought as she looked around and saw the same perplexed look on the other attendees faces.

 A few more seconds went by, then Bishop put up the third and final picture.

"This is definitely a picture of an outside garage or carport" Priscilla wrote without hesitation. She also thought the significance was that you could drive right through. Perhaps this is a depiction of Church on Sunday. Most people do whatever they want to do during the week, then drive through Church on Sunday morning, get a little Word in you, then cruise on back to doing whatever makes one happy. At that moment, Priscilla began thinking….we didn't need to come to a conference to be told we could continue doing what we've always been doing. If that's the case, we wouldn't be in this room searching for JOY. Just as Priscilla started looking around to see the faces of others, Bishop Justice proclaimed again the word "JOY". It was almost as if he used the word to get our attention…. "Interesting", she thought.

He then asked the attendees to do something that Priscilla always dreads. Bishop asked that the attendees form a three-person group (with people we don't know) and write down their responses to their first impression about the pictures. She unwillingly picked up her paper and was obedient. 😳

Priscilla looked around the room to find two other people that were in her age range. To her surprise there weren't many in the room that looked younger than 40. Just as she had that thought an energetic young lady tapped her on the shoulder and said "Hi, my name is Lisa, and this is Sandy. Would you like to join us?" Priscilla immediately said "Sure!". After all, they were probably the only people in the session of 50 that were still in their twenties. Ironically, they all had the same response – Carport/Garage – for picture number one. For picture number 2 Sandy stated, "it is an elongated upside-down ice cream cone". Priscilla and Lisa both looked at Sandy as if she was crazy but both ladies said in unison "Okay". Lisa proceeded to share that she wrote a house. Priscilla commentated that she originally wrote house but marked it out because the roof was too big and wrote the shapes. When the ladies transitioned to the third picture, Sandy stated it is the letter U. Lisa immediately spoke up and said "Yeah, I see it, it does look like the letter U. But, I wrote that it was an upside-down table." Priscilla then shared, "that is amazing because I also wrote an upside-down table." Instantly, Priscilla thought that her and this Lisa chick may have more similarities than just their age.

With that thought the ladies' attention was then turned by the familiar booming voice proclaiming "JOY". The ladies knew their time for discussion was up. Bishop Justice had placed the original picture of all three shapes back on the board and asked the groups to take 2 minutes to compare and contrast the three pictures.

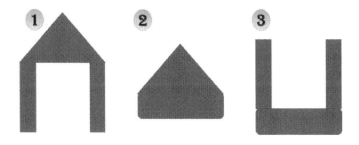

When the 2-minute timer went off, Bishop said, "When we look at these three pictures each of us may see different things and that is typically based on our previous experiences. But something interesting should happen when you look at all three pictures simultaneously. As I was walking around the room listening to the group discussions, the group of young ladies in the back hit the nail on the head." He was pointing to the three ladies, (Lisa, Sandy, and Priscilla). "Ladies, will one of you please share your observation of these three pictures?" At that moment Lisa, in the most outgoing fashion, stood up and proclaimed, "each picture seemed to be missing a piece that the other picture possessed. The first picture is missing the base, the second is missing the middle, and the third is missing the top."

Bishop Justice emphatically stated, "That's absolutely correct young lady. It typically takes attendees a few minutes to make the distinction; however, these ladies identified the difference instantly. In fact, the actual picture that represents JOY with all pieces completely intact looks like this." Bishop then shows a picture of a house with a heart on the inside. He proceeded to explain, "The reason why we did this exercise in viewing the shapes was to see how easy it is to be perceived as being whole, being healed, being happy, being complete when we don't have something to compare or contrast. Now that you see the complete house, it is easy to identify the missing pieces of the previous pictures, Right?" Just about all the attendees are shaking their heads in agreement. Some of them even whispered to their neighbors…. "that does make sense". By this time, Bishop Justice had made his way back to the front of the room.

Priscilla whispered to her new friend Lisa, "This all sounds good but what exactly does this have to do with JOY?" At that moment, something happened that shook the base of Priscilla's being.

Bishop Justice look directly at Priscilla and said, "I'm so glad you asked that question young lady." Everyone in the session from the front of the room to the back of the room, which is where Priscilla's group was still sitting, was wondering who asked a question because no one said anything.

Priscilla thought to herself, why is he looking at me. He couldn't have possibly heard what I asked Lisa. And at that moment Bishop repeated word for word what Priscilla asked.

Bishop quoted, "The young lady in the back stated that this all sounds good but what exactly does this have to do with JOY?"

No one in the room seem phased by the revelation of the Bishop, probably because they had the same question. However, Priscilla was amazed that he knew exactly what she said. She realized that she was the only one in amazement so just as quickly as she had the suspicious feeling she dismissed it as a mere coincidence.

Bishop continued "This is a great segue to the purpose of this session. To be an Effective Leader, you must lead with JOY which means to have all three components of the house. The base or the foundation of the house is the J which stands for Jesus. The structure of the house is the O which stands for Others. And finally, the roof of the house is the Y which stands for You. My sessions today and Part 2 on tomorrow will focus on the foundation of the house which is what's missing with the first picture. The foundation is the actual supporting structure of a house so it is only fitting to begin at the beginning."

Priscilla then began thinking this is starting to make sense and as soon as she had that thought she side eyed Bishop to see if he was going to say anything about what she just thought. When he didn't say anything, she thought maybe the fact that he knew what she was thinking before was just a one-time thing. Now she was getting excited all over again about finding JOY.

She gave Bishop her undivided attention as she heard him say "The path to true JOY starts just like the first step of the actual building process of a house…..THE FOUNDATION. In your three person groups, I want you to write down what you think is needed to lay the foundation of a house. You have 3 minutes to both discuss and write your thoughts down. GO"

Sandy spoke up first, "my dad actually builds houses and he is always talking about the importance of the foundation of a house. In fact, he mentions that the footings are first created with wood like stakes before the concrete is poured."

Lisa said, "Wow, I didn't know that. I just assumed that concrete was just poured then the bricks or concrete blocks were added around them."

Priscilla commented, "I have no idea. I put my trust in the building inspectors and if it passes I move in."

All three ladies laughed as the Bishop hollered "JOY". He then asked for a couple of groups to report out their thoughts. Most groups shared the same information that Priscilla's group discussed.

Then one of the conference attendants came in the room and announced that they have 10 minutes left in the session.

Priscilla thought, "Wow, that was a quick 45 minutes."

Bishop then showed a picture on the board of an animated guy standing beside the foundation of a house. He agreed that there are three main materials needed for a proper foundation. These three materials are plywood, steel, and concrete. Bishop explained, "The plywood represents Hope, the steel represents Faith, and the concrete represents Love. These three materials or ingredients are vital in having a strong relationship with Jesus which is CRUCIAL when you are in a position of leadership. Therefore, the driving scripture for J in Joy comes from 1 Corinthians 13:13. And it reads from the NKJV, 'And now abide faith, hope, love, these three; but the greatest of these *is* love.'"

Bishop then declared, "We have only scratched the surface of JOY Leadership. I encourage each of you to come back to my session tomorrow for the meat of the letter J. Be sure to come early as it looks like the session fills up quickly. Enjoy the rest of today and I will see you tomorrow same time same place."

Priscilla bided the two ladies farewell and dashed to get her daughter so that she could go home to get ready for the night's events. After all, it is Friday and the day was young!!!

CHAPTER TWO

Priscilla dropped her daughter off at her godmother's house and raced to the house to get dressed up for the night's festivities. She only had one hour to get in her best outfit and meet her girls so that they could travel to Pride University. Pride was the closest HBCU to Priscilla's alma mater, Grace University. When she was attending the school, she and her girls would always go to Pride to support their annual step shows. Tonight, was a special step show where they had been asked to do a few strolls at the after party. It was also important to Priscilla, because there was a special someone that had been trying, for years, to get her to go on a date with him. But Steve, her baby daddy, was always in the picture.

Speaking of Steve, she hadn't heard from him all day. In fact, she hadn't spoken to him since Wednesday morning. It is now Friday at 5:00pm. Most people would consider that strange; however, Priscilla was beginning to see the bigger picture.

She had become a statistic......Boy meets girl, girl doesn't really like boy, boy woos girl, girl becomes interested in boy, boy takes advantage of girl, girl gets pregnant, boy finds new love interests.

If you were to ask Steve, he would say he loves Priscilla and most definitely his baby girl. If you asked Priscilla, she would say Steve loved her if she was helping him out financially and physically. But every time he got back on his feet financially, he helped himself physically in other places.

Priscilla often wondered why her girls didn't like Steve. She had been dating him for 3 years and although they were always cordial with him, you could tell they didn't want her to date him. She was clueless until after their child was born and she assumed that she would move in with him. Since she just had a baby, she didn't have an opportunity to search for a job in her academic field. So, she settled for a paycheck. A very very small paycheck. With little money coming in, she thought that they would save more if she moved in with him, after all each time he was unemployed he lived with her. But that wasn't going to be the case. Steve insisted that it would be better if "Cilla" moved into her own apartment. In fact, he found her the perfect place, according to Steve. Being the naive, head over heels, "stupid" female that she was, she agreed to live in this "perfect place". By the way, the perfect place was 15 miles away from the city limits. Yes, the place was nice, and it was extremely reasonably priced. However, whenever she would ask if Steve was coming to visit, he would conveniently say he was tired from work and it was a "long drive". WHAT?????? And of course, if Priscilla ever suspected anything, she would have to find childcare to catch him in the act. But who has time for that when you are busy being a working single mother? So, although she suspected things weren't good, she elected to continue to be in a relationship with him.

Enough about Steve, it was time to meet the girls. She rolled into the parking lot of her girlfriend Sheila's apartment on two wheels. It looked like everyone was already in the SUV. They were just waiting on Priscilla. She hopped in the front seat and the ladies were off to their destination.

Sheila asked, "what music do y'all want me to play?" Priscilla popped in a new cassette tape that she had just received from a co-worker. It was Kirk Franklin's "Melodies from Heaven". Donna, who also recently had a child, hollers from the back, "Girl if you don't take that tape out. What we look like listening to gospel music on the way to sin?" Priscilla said, "We need this covering the way Sheila is driving!" Sheila then said, "I wouldn't have to drive so fast, if you weren't so late." Then everyone agreed that they should listen to TLC's "Waterfalls". They all sang in unison ….. "Don't go chasing waterfalls……"

The step show was amazing!!! And as always, the devastating ladies from Grace University set the party out with their undeniable precision and finesse. After the after party the ladies stayed for a few more hours hanging with the brothers laughing, dancing, and doing what most recently graduated college students do.

It was now about 3:30 in the morning, well past time to go home. Most of the girls were somewhat inebriated, so it was up to the non-drinkers, Priscilla or Jennifer, to see them home safely. Priscilla yielded to Jennifer since she was still determined to go to the second session with Bishop Justice that would be starting in about 5 hours.

Thirty minutes into the ride home Priscilla was wakened by what she thought was pot holes in the road, only to find out that Jennifer had fallen asleep. She yelled out, "Jennifer wake up." Jennifer jumped and declared in a sleepy voice, "Giiiiirrrrlll, I'm not sleep. I was just resting my eyelids for a second." Hearing the commotion everyone woke up and was seemingly sober. Sheila asked, "Who in the hell let Jennifer drive my truck? Y'all know she will fall asleep in a minute." With that, Jennifer pulled the truck over and switched seats with Priscilla. Once they got to Sheila's house, the ladies agreed they had another story that they vowed to keep between them as they hugged good night.

Priscilla rose from a total of 2 hours sleep and realized she was supposed to pick up her daughter this morning. But if she did, she would be late for Bishop Justice's session that was going to start promptly at 9:00 am. She called her daughter's godmother to see if she could stay for a few more hours, while she attended the session at church. All she had to do was mention the word church, cause God mommy had been preaching salvation since she found out Priscilla was pregnant. Once she got the okay, she quickly showered, got dressed, and headed to the church.

God was definitely at work as Priscilla was told once again that she was the last one they were going to let into the room. Once again, the session was packed and she slid in the last available seat but this time it was in the front of the room.

Bishop Justice enters the room from the back and roars the word "JOY". He then asked if anyone remembers the meaning of the last picture that he displayed prior to ending the session yesterday.   Several hands went up, while Priscilla's head went down. She felt him standing beside her as Bishop emphatically asked, "How about you young lady? Please share with us what you remember about this picture." He was pointing to the picture that was displayed on the screen.

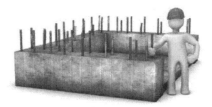

Priscilla wanted so desperately to say call on someone else, but the words wouldn't come out of her mouth. Instead she pulled out her notes and stated, "The picture is the foundation of a house which we learned consists of three main ingredients which are wood, steal, and concrete. These three ingredients can be compared to the three main ingredients of Hope, Faith, and Love which are important, to have a strong foundation in Jesus." As soon as Priscilla finished talking, she felt sweat on her palms, rolling down her forehead, and on her back all at once.

Bishop declared, "That my friends is the **J** in **JOY**. Great job young lady, I knew you were paying attention yesterday!" He continued saying, "At the beginning of the class yesterday, I shared three pictures that were each missing a piece that would complete our House of JOY. The picture displayed on the screen now is a house that lacks a strong foundation. A person without a solid spiritual foundation has no REAL relationship with Jesus. They may appear to be generally good people but they lack genuine hope, faith, and love. Without these ingredients, it is impossible to be an effective leader."

Bishop continued, "Let's start first with the plywood. According to the website 'Understanding Building Construction' plywood is described as an economical, factory-produced sheet of wood with precise dimensions that does not warp or crack with changes in atmospheric moisture." Bishop paused, placed his finger on his head as if he was thinking. He continued, "Remember these words, economical, precise, and crack. The purpose of the plywood in building a house is to establish the frame in which the cement would be poured into. We equate the plywood in the construction of a house's foundation with Hope in building a spiritual foundation. I often use the Life Application Study Bible when doing research and in the commentary for 1 Corinthians 13:13 it states that Hope is an attitude and focus. In other words, a person must first make up their mind that they believe and focus their attention on what is important. When I thought about that commentary, it led me to a 3-step process for Hope that fits well in building our foundational relationship with Jesus. The first step is Salvation. Romans 10:9 states 'that if you confess with your mouth the Lord Jesus and believe in your heart that God has raised Him from the dead, you will be saved.' So, we must first have an attitude of salvation by confessing with our mouths and believing in our hearts."

Just as Bishop was quoting the scripture from Romans, Priscilla looked down at her paper and thought about the first of the three words he asked them to remember – economical. She recalled her great aunt always saying that salvation is free.

Bishop continued, "The second step is understanding eternal life. 1 John 5:13-14 declares, 'These things I have written to you who believe in the name of the Son of God, that you may know that you have eternal life, and that you may continue *to* believe in the name of the Son of God.' If we believe in God which is what we confess when we are saved, then we will have eternal life. Then the third step is realizing that there will be light afflictions. According to 2 Corinthians 4:16-18 'Therefore we do not lose heart. Even though our outward man is perishing, yet the inward man is being renewed day by day. For our light affliction, which is but for a moment, is working for us a far more exceeding and eternal weight of glory.' We must remain strong in our hope that even though things happen in our lives that may not feel good at the moment, it is only temporary."

He then put up a chart that illustrated the comparison of the plywood as it relates to the purpose of Hope in building a strong spiritual foundation.

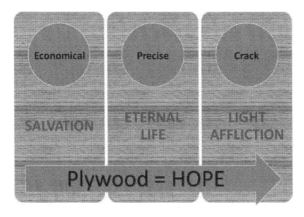

You could hear the agreement in the audience as they began to talk to their neighbors. Many said, "this makes sense." Others replied, "never thought about it that way".

Bishop Justice didn't want the audience to miss the importance of his explanation. "Salvation is the most economical thing you will ever receive on this earth. Jesus paid the price thousands of years ago so that you can have the most precise outcome to your life which is to have it eternally. However, we must realize that there will be a few cracks, called afflictions, along the way. However, when we focus our attention on the promise (that the afflictions are only temporary) the process becomes easier to bare." He paused for a moment and realized that hands were going up everywhere.

His reply, "guys we must go on because I don't want to run out of time. We still have to discuss the steel and the concrete portions of the foundation. I promise I will leave time for questions at the end of the session."

"Steel Rebar" Bishop insistently continued, "is commonly used to strengthen concrete. Rebar is made from different alloys and grades of steel and is manufactured with ridges so that the concrete that is poured onto the bars can adhere easily to them. Its purpose is to prevent cracks and possible leaks. Similarly, that's what faith does for the Christian Leader. Strong faith prevents negative thoughts or negative people from cracking your spiritual foundation. Chapter 11 in Hebrews is considered by most bible scholars as the faith chapter. In this chapter, it defines faith as the substance (or confidence) of things hoped for and the evidence of things not seen."

Steel Rebar = FAITH

At this point in the session, Priscilla could feel her adrenaline leave her body and her eyelids getting extremely heavy. What happened to the movement and excitement of the session the day before. Just as she had that thought she heard Bishop ask for a volunteer. And a somewhat familiar voice in the middle of the room say, "me, me, me". It was Lisa. One of the ladies that was in her 3-person group from the previous day.

Bishop placed a chair in the front of the room and asked Lisa to stand in front of the chair and look towards the audience. After she positioned herself, he asked her to sit down. Lisa looked back at the chair then sat down. Bishop said, "Okay, now I want you to stand back up and look at the audience while you sit in the chair." This time Lisa felt for the chair as she was sitting down. The audience along with Bishop laughed as he stated, "Now I want you to stand back up, look at the audience, and hold your hands above your head while you sit in the chair." When Lisa sat in the chair without looking or touching, Bishop stated, "That's NOW Faith. Now if I were to call each of you to do the same, most of you wouldn't have to be told to look at the audience and hold your hands up, because you would have the faith that the chair would not only be behind you, but also that the chair would keep you from falling. That is the faith that God wants us to have in Him. Thank you, young lady, you may be seated. Let's give her a hand for volunteering."

Priscilla was ever so thankful for the moment of amusement as it gave her a little energy to stay attentive.

Then Bishop stated, "It doesn't take a lot of faith to be effective. According to Mathew in chapter 17 verse 20, faith the size of a mustard seed (which is smaller than a poppy seed) enables you to command a mountain to move from one location to another and it would be done. There is nothing impossible for you to do when done in the name of Jesus. But there are a few prerequisites to having such faith. One very important one is, You must study!!! Just like Paul told his protégé Timothy in 2 Timothy 2:15 you must 'study to present yourself approved to God, a worker who does not need to be ashamed, rightly dividing the word of truth.' In an effort to have a strong foundation it is important that you have the content knowledge. You must understand who God is and how He operates. In order to have the understanding, it is imperative that you spend time in the

Word of God. Simply put, you need to STUDY and your faith will be as strong as Steel Rebar."

Finally, Bishop stated, "The most important ingredient or material for a strong foundation of a house is Concrete. You could have the best plywood and the strongest Rebar but without concrete, there would be no foundation. The same is true Spiritually. A person can have the right focus and believe the Word of God; however, without Love there is no foundation. In fact, 1 Corinthians 13:2 tells us '...if we have all the faith to remove mountains, without love we are Nothing!'

Priscilla could tell that Bishop was rushing so she took a peak at her watch to see that he was down to about 10 minutes. Then the conference attendant walked in and told him just that. "Bishop you have 10 minutes left."

Bishop gasped and said, "Wow! Time flies when you are having fun. I promised you all time for questions, but I have 3 points about love that I must make. First is the definition of Love that can be found in 1 Corinthians 13:4-7....in summary Love is kind, it endures, not proud, not rude, not provoked, not evil, nor selfish. Love is so important that when God gave the first two commandments to Moses they were about love. According to Mathew 22:37-39, the first commandment is to Love God and the second is to Love your neighbor as yourself. Lastly, we couldn't possibly discuss Love without referencing John 3:16. God loved us so much that he sacrificed his perfect son Jesus. This is the type of Love that lays a strong, concrete like, foundation that produces Highly Effective Leaders!!! Just in case you didn't get the scriptures they are here on the screen. Now, what questions do you have?"

PART TWO – OTHERS (the structure)

CHAPTER THREE

As Priscilla drove home after the conference, she reflected on her newfound knowledge of JOY. She thought she would be miraculously in a different place within herself. While she was at the conference, she felt a peace that was indescribable, but as she began to think about what she had to do the rest of the evening the peace / JOY seemed to slowly ooze out of her body.

At that point, she thought about the last question that was asked before they departed. Her new friend Lisa asked, "In the beginning you mentioned that there were three parts to JOY. How can you leave us hanging with only providing us with the J? Do you have a handout about the other two letters? At the very least tell us how to get the information on the O and the Y."

Bishop then smiled and responded, "I was wondering who was going to ask that question. There are details about all three pieces to Leading with Joy in my books. They are for sale out in the corridor where the vendors are set up. Also, at my vendor booth, I will have a list of my upcoming conference presentations. In fact, my next conference is on the campus of Pride University next month and I will be presenting on the O (Others) section. Registration is free to college students; however, my session will only hold 30 people so register early.

While driving to work the following Monday, Priscilla noticed Bishop's flyer with the picture of Pride University that was on the seat beside her and said out loud, "I must go to the post office when I get off to register for the conference."

The rest of the week, Priscilla continued her normal routine of getting her bundle of joy ready for daycare, dropping her off, going to work, picking her up, then doing their normal nighttime ritual. Steve would call to see if they had a good day. Priscilla would feed the baby, take a bath, and off to sleep.

Three weeks went by and one day something very strange occurred. She was riding down the road and felt the irritating urge to throw up. She pulled over abruptly and "tossed all her cookies". In that instance, she recalled that she questioned whether the chicken sat out too long prior to cooking it for dinner the night before. So, she dismissed the stomach irritation she felt all day for possible food poisoning. What she found to be odd was the fact that she was sick the entire week, but nothing was going to keep her from going to the conference that Bishop Justice was facilitating at Pride University this Saturday.

As she was getting out of her car at Pride, she noticed a familiar face getting out of a car three spaces over. It was Lisa. Lisa ran over to Priscilla and said, "Girl, I was hoping you were going to be here. Let's hurry up so we can be sure to get into Bishop Justice's session."

The two ladies walked swiftly to the registration desk then to the small auditorium for the opening session of the conference. As soon as they announced the location for Bishop Justice's session they jumped up and headed to the room to sit in the front of the room. To their surprise, there were already a dozen people in the room. They elected to sit in the middle as close to the front as they could. After about 10 minutes they heard a familiar roar, "JOY!"

Bishop Justice entered the room in signature fashion. He announced to the world that this was the place to find the JOY in Leadership. At that moment, he directed the class to do an icebreaker activity. He asked everyone to take the piece of paper on their table and answer the three questions displayed on the board. After 3 minutes, he asked the audience to find 2 people that they didn't know and discuss their answers.

1. Do you LOVE Everyone?

2. What type of people are easy to LOVE?

3. What type of people are more difficult to LOVE?

Priscilla found a young lady that was across the room that made eye contact with her; however, as she was walking towards the lady a masculine voice said with uncertainty, "Priscilla?" She turned around quickly and recognized the face. Her heart began beating hysterically, as her eyes bulged from her head and immediately her mind shifted to a few short weeks ago when she was on the yard of Pride University. When her voice caught up with her thoughts she asked, "what are you doing here?" Before he could respond, she rushed out of the room and darted to the nearest bathroom where she could relieve herself of everything she ate that morning. Almost too embarrassed to return to the room, she cleaned herself, rinsed her mouth out, popped in a piece of gum, held her head up, and marched back to the room. At this time Bishop was telling the attendees that time was up and to return to their seats.

Lisa asked Priscilla, "where did you go?" Priscilla responded that she would tell her about it after the session. She tried hard to focus on Bishop, but all she could think about was why the guy that she spent most of the night with after the step show a few weeks back was at the same conference, in the same session as her. But wait, he was still a student there. She had to encourage herself to get it together and focus.

Bishop asked the attendees to raise their hand if they can honestly say that they LOVE everyone. As people began to raise their hands, he immediately told them to put their hands down. Then he said, "Raise your hand if you love your mother." Just about all hands went up. Before he gave his next direction, he stated that this is strictly hypothetical. Then he said, "Raise your hand if we would love the person, Lord forbid, that shot and killed your mother." There was not one hand that went up. "That's what I thought."

He proceeded, "That's why I asked the question. It is clearly a lot easier to love those that love us, but when people don't express love, it becomes a lot more challenging. In today's 2-part session, we will discuss the importance of Others in our journey to become a Leader who leads with JOY. For those of you who have attended my session on J you may recall seeing this picture." He pointed to the board that displayed the picture that was missing the middle of the house.

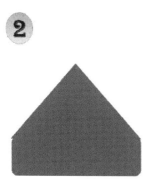

Bishop continued, "This picture represents a house that has a foundation and a roof but is missing the main part.

The structure of the house is typically the place where you would spend majority of your time. The truth is we spend majority of our time with other people whether it is at work, home, church, or school. Therefore, it is imperative that we have a good grip on how to interact with others in order to have JOY. Let's break the structure of the house into two main parts. There are the joists (floor & ceiling) and the Walls (load bearing and exterior). See the location of these parts in the picture on the screen."

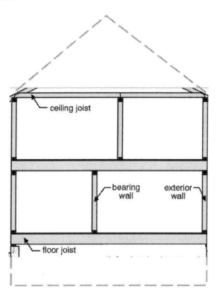

He then asked the attendees to go to 1 Corinthians 3:10 – 14 and asked for a volunteer to read. Hands went up but he called on a familiar face. "Young lady in the middle with the red button up shirt. Please read."

Priscilla looked down at her shirt and realized he was talking about her. She began to read...

> "¹⁰ According to the grace of God which was given to me, as a wise master builder I have laid the foundation, and another builds on it. But let each one take heed how he builds on it. ¹¹ For no other foundation can anyone lay than that which is laid, which is Jesus Christ. ¹² Now if anyone builds on this foundation *with* gold, silver, precious stones, wood, hay, straw, ¹³ each one's work will become clear; for the Day will declare it, because it will be revealed by fire; and the fire will test each one's work, of what sort it is. ¹⁴ If anyone's work which he has built on *it* endures, he will receive a reward."
> 1 Corinthians 3:10-14 NKJV

Upon the completion of Priscilla reading the scripture, Bishop yells out "Woooooo that sums up this session. This is our driving scripture for the letter O. The foundation, which is Jesus, is discussed in detail during my session on J. If you haven't attended that session, please see me during lunch to find out more information. But it is what goes on the foundation that we are going to talk about in detail today. Let's continue by looking at verse 12 that lists the items that man could use to build on top of its foundation."

Bishop put his finger on his head as if to show he was deep in thought. He then reflected, "I recall when I first read this scripture, several years ago, I connected it to the old nursery rhyme about the little three pigs. Everyone remembers that story, how the wolf would try to get inside the pig's home by huffing and puffing until he could blow the house down. The three houses were made of hay, straw, and bricks. So, it is with this scripture. In Paul's writing to the people of Corinth, he is telling them that it is their decision on what to build their houses with. He starts with the sturdiest materials (less flammable) and ends with the most brittle (more flammable). Paul then continues to inform the people that each man's work would be tested by fire (tests or trials) and whatever remains after the fire is what will stand. That brings us to the question on how can we stand the test of the fire? That my friends is the million-dollar question."

Priscilla was trying so hard to focus on the information that was being shared, but she couldn't help but think about her guy friend that was sitting a few seats behind her. She quickly remembered that Bishop was prone to calling on her at any moment so she had to keep it together.

Pointing back to the illustration of the house with the four parts, Bishop declares, "Let's get back to the parts of the structure that I referenced before. The joists and the walls. We will cover the joists before lunch and the walls after lunch. The joists represent love. This love is a continuation of the love that was laid in the foundation of the house which is what was discussed in the J session. According to Wisegeek.com, the floor joists are important to stability and security of the floor. The joists provide support in order to do what it was made to do. The floor joist is a structural example of the scripture John 15:13." At that point, Bishop took a long pause.

As Bishop paused, Priscilla completely forgot about the gentleman sitting behind her for a brief minute. And immediately read the verse to herself and jolted her arm in the air to ask a question.

Bishop greeted her with a smirk on his face, "yes ma'am?"

Priscilla asked, "I may be jumping way ahead, but you mean to tell me that in order to have a solid structure, I must be willing to die for others?" She looked at Bishop as if to say, you must be crazy.

Bishop then asked her to read the verse right before aloud. She complied.

> "This is My commandment, that you love one
> another as I have loved you"
> John 15:12 NKJV

After reading the scripture she gave the Bishop a smile, acknowledging the fact that God commands us to love just like he loves us.

Bishop told the crowd, "In order to be an effective leader, it is a must that you love everyone, but especially the people that you have been given authority over. So yes, you are to sacrifice yourself for the sake of others. I realize that this sounds like a lot; however, if we backed up one more scripture to John 15:11, it tells us this is what we must do to be full of JOY. It's kind of like the ceiling joists. Wisegeek.com explains that the ceiling joist is what brings the walls together in preparation for the ceiling. So, it is with LOVE. It brings everyone together when we approach each situation with the attitude that we will die for someone else. A wise woman once said, "that we should love everyone the way that most good mothers love their children."

While Bishop was talking, a young lady from the back of the room passed out sheets of paper.

Bishop then explained the activity that attendees will be asked to complete. He stated, "The objective of this session is for each attendee to be able to effectively lead others with a heart of JOY. In order to successfully accomplish this goal, we are going to break up in groups of 3 to 4. Each group will be given a scenario that could happen in the workplace. You are to draft a 60 second skit on how you would handle the assigned scenario. You will have the remainder of this session and the entire hour and ½ lunch break to work on your skit. The instructions are on the sheet passed out. Please select your group members and I will come around to deliver your scenario."

Of course, Priscilla and Lisa were in the same group. They solicited the help from the female that was sitting on the opposite side of Lisa.

As Bishop walked by the ladies, he said, "I have the perfect scenario for you three." He handed them a slip of paper.

> **Scenario #12**
>
> A female director of a call center has to decide how to handle a situation between two female employees. The first female employee is very confident, has a strong personality, and only has a few friends in the department. The other female employee is very shy and insecure, but gets along well with others. The confident employee witness the shy employee stealing. The confident employee goes to the shy employee to tell her what she saw. The shy employee is furious and goes to the boss to tell her that she feels bullied by the confident employee. How should the director handle this situation?

The three ladies read over the scenario and wondered how they were going to address this situation. They discussed the fact that one employee was probably not liked because she was a know it all. Lisa stated, "I imagine the shy employee is liked because she doesn't bother anybody." Priscilla said, "she sounds sneaky to me". The other female in the group asked if she could be the director in the skit, she also volunteered to write out the skit. Lisa and Priscilla looked at each other and gave a unanimous, "sure!" At that moment Lisa asked Priscilla what was going on with her earlier. Priscilla shared the details of her last visit to Pride University and about her encounter with the guy in the back of the room.

Fifteen minutes passed and they heard a voice come over the intercom stating that lunch was being served in the commons area. Bishop Justice announced to the class that they would resume the second part of the session promptly at 1:30.

CHAPTER FOUR

"Girl, you are pregnant!" exclaimed Lisa. Priscilla spit out pieces of her sandwich that she was eating for lunch then shouted, "No ma'am, I have a baby at home that is less than a year old. There is no way in the world that I could be pregnant AGAIN!"

At that moment Priscilla got very quiet as she thought about the last few weeks. "The feelings I've had the last few days were very similar to the time I found out about my bundle of joy. But, how could this be possible? Steve and I really haven't been intimate on a regular basis since the baby was born." She dismissed the thought and turned to her friend and said, "This is just the stomach flu, it has been going around on my job. I have the same symptoms as a few other ladies in my office." She then insisted that they go back and work on the skit. After all they left ALL the work up to the other young lady.

As they walked back to the room, Priscilla asked, "What is the name of the young lady we are working with?" Lisa shrugged her shoulders and said, "I'm not sure, but we need to find out. We are the worst partners. We aren't illustrating love at all. We must do better!"

Priscilla turned to head towards the room and was startled in such a way that a little pee ran down her leg. It was the guy from the back of the room. The guy that she was trying so hard to avoid. The guy that she spent a few hours alone with that night she was hanging with the girls.

"Gerald, you scared me!" she exclaimed.

He responded, "Why are you avoiding me? I thought we were cool?"

"We are cool. I just wasn't expecting to see you here today. I know you went to school here, but don't you work in another state?" Priscilla questioned.

"Yes, I live about two hours away, but my boy was telling me about Bishop, so I wanted to check him out. Everything he said was true, he's legit," Gerald explained.

Priscilla responded, "Yeah, no doubt. But I need to get back to my group so we can finish our skit. I'll catch up with you another time." She scurried away heading back to the ladies that were waiting for her.

Back in the room, Lisa questioned Priscilla, "Was that him? Was that the guy that you were telling me about?" She lowered her voice and whispered in Priscilla's ear, "Did you tell him you are pregnant?"

Priscilla gave Lisa a scathing look and said emphatically, "I AM NOT!!!" She then lowered her voice and pleaded, "Let's get back to work, please."

The three ladies came up with a phenomenal skit that portrayed the Director in a loving compassionate way, handling the situation with Solomon wisdom. They wrote that the director would give the two ladies an option where only the person that was not telling the truth would accept. This way she would be forced to reprimand the employee that was truly dishonest. The conference attendees gave them a standing ovation for their thoughtful approach to a delicate situation.

Bishop then recapped the first part of the session with a chart that was projected on the screen.

House Structure	Physical Purpose	Spiritual Structure	Spiritual Purpose
JOISTS (Floor and Ceiling)	**Floor Joists** – important to the stability and security of the floor. Installed in the early stages of the flooring. **Ceiling Joists** - to tie the rooms/walls together making a box and to lay a foundation for the ceiling	LOVE John 15:10 - 15	Stability • Complete Joy Security • Commandment to love others = friends of God Sacrifice • Lay down life

He continued, "Now that we understand the joists part of the structure, let's focus our attention on the walls. To refresh your memory, here is the picture shown earlier illustrating the load bearing and exterior walls."

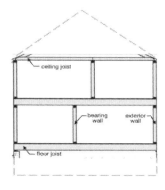

Bishop asked the attendees to explain in their own words what they think a bearing wall was. Several hands went up. He called on Gerald in the back. Gerald said, "It is a wall that bears the load of a structure above it. My grandpa taught me at an early age that if I took on a big task I needed to be sure that I could bear the load. He compared it to a load bearing wall in the center of our house. In fact, he described how us boys would rough house upstairs. If the wall underneath wasn't strong enough to carry the load, the floor would collapse, and we would ultimately be downstairs." As he described his grandpa's explanation, Gerald made a London Bridge is falling down type of gesture.

Several people including Bishop laughed. Not Priscilla. She had other thoughts running through her head as she reflected back on the time she spent with Gerald a few weeks back.

Gerald stated, "That's how he explained it."

Bishop shook his head in affirmation and stated, "that's exactly right young man. A load bearing wall is described by NaturalHandyMan.com as a wall securing the intersection of joists or beams. See the example on the screen."

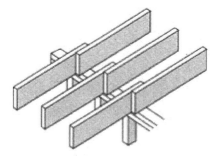

He continued, "If it weren't for the bearing wall, the beams wouldn't be secure. And as the young guy just mentioned, any rough housing or excessive weight would cause the floor to come down. The load bearing wall for a structure is like the Holy Spirit for man. If we don't have the Holy Spirit within us, it would be very difficult for us to maintain the Hope, Faith, and Love that was laid at the foundation of our relationship with Jesus. In fact, before Jesus was crucified, He informed his followers that when He left, He would send a comforter and that comforter is the Holy Spirit. Romans 8:26 tells the reader that the Spirit helps our weakness, just like the load bearing wall helps the weak parts of a structure."

Lisa whispered into Priscilla's ear, "What in the world does this have to do with how to interact with others?"

Priscilla looked weirdly at Lisa and responded, "What are you talking about?"

With a puzzled look Lisa asked, "What's wrong with you? Didn't you hear what Bishop just explained?"

"No, I guess I was in my own little world." Priscilla admitted.

Lisa firmly stated, "You need to focus on what is important at this moment. We will deal with the other situation after this session. After all, you pressed your way to get here so let's learn as much as we can."

Priscilla agreed and placed her undivided attention back on Bishop.

Bishop noticed the two young ladies talking. He leaned his head to the side and raised one of his eyebrows to express recognition as if he were their father commanding them to pay attention. He then went on with his next thought. "I sense that you all are wondering how the Holy Spirit is connected to how we interact with others so let's do a brief illustration.

May I have the gentleman in the back that provided the detailed illustration about his grandfather." Bishop motioned for Gerald to come up front. "And I also want my friend Ms. Priscilla, that is your name, right?" Priscilla shook her head in the affirmative and hesitantly moved to the front of the room.

Bishop picked up a bandanna from the table and asked Priscilla to put the bandanna over her eyes like a blind fold. Recognizing that Priscilla was somewhat hesitant, he said to her "Just trust me, it will be okay."

She put the blindfold on and couldn't see a thing.

Then Bishop asked her to walk to the back of the room, turn right then walk back to the front of the room.

Priscilla responded, "But I can't see anything".

Bishop then asked Gerald to take Priscilla's hand and walk her to the back of the room, turn right then walk her back to the front of the room. He said, "Make sure that she doesn't hit anything, but is safely guided back to the front of the room."

After the illustration was complete, Bishop explained the illustration. "This is what the Holy Spirit does for a Christian. If you are sensitive to the Holy Spirit, He will guide you where you need to go. Let's look at a couple more scriptures. Galatians 5:25 tells us we need to '…. WALK by the Spirit'. 1 Corinthians 2:13 informs the reader that we should speak words taught by the Spirit and not by human wisdom. And finally, Mathew 16:17 where Jesus is telling Peter that his knowledge wasn't revealed to him by flesh and blood (human nature) but by the Father… in essence the Holy Spirit."

Bishop told everyone to close their eyes and focus on the last time they had an interaction with another person that didn't go so well. He proceeded, "Now think about how better the interaction would have gone had you been led by the Holy Spirit. That my friend is the load bearing wall in your life. It is imperative that you yield to the Holy Spirit's guidance in your interaction with others."

Priscilla was still standing in the front of the room when she raised her hand then blurted out, "But how do you know that it's the Holy Spirit and not just your own feelings or thoughts?"

"That is a great question." Bishop responded "In fact, let's talk about that for a moment. I realize that we have a room full of people at various points in their relationship with Christ. So, we are going to pause right now and quickly discuss salvation and if there is anyone in the room that isn't saved, we can lead you through the plan of salvation today."

After several minutes and a few souls saved Bishop declared, "Wow, I didn't expect that, but this is an amazingly unplanned illustration of allowing the Holy Spirit to guide your footsteps. Today we together won a few more souls for the Kingdom of God. Now going back to the question that was asked. Let's refer to the scripture Acts 2:38 when Peter informed the Israelites that if they repent and be baptized, they would receive the gift of the Holy Spirit. So, once you are saved you will receive the Holy Spirit. Then just like anything else, you must spend time in the Word of God and fellowshipping with believers to strengthen your personal relationship with Christ. When you do this, you will be in tune with the Holy Spirit and will know when it is the Spirit and not just your own ..... how did you put it ..... feelings or thoughts. Does this answer your question young lady?"

Priscilla nodded in the affirmative, but quickly began to think about the things that she had done that may not be lined up with the word of God. In fact, she had a visible witness right in the room. It was at that moment that she felt extremely sorrowful almost to the point of tears. She had to pull herself together because they had at least another 40 minutes to go in the session. She and several others returned to their seats after having witnessed a mighty move of God.

Bishop started again, "Time check" he looked at his watch. "We have about 30 minutes remaining. That's just enough time for us to cover the Exterior Walls. We defined the meaning of the interior load bearing wall and its spiritual purpose being the Holy Spirit. Just remember that like the interior load bearing wall it can't always be seen but you can tell if it's not present. Now let's transition to the outer walls. This is the wall that most people see. I like to call these walls, judgement. Because if the outer walls look good then people will assume that the inside is good. When my wife and I were looking for our first house we found what we thought was the perfect house. It looked great from the street and the price was phenomenal. But when we called the realtor, he told us that we didn't want to buy the house because we would need to put at least $100,000 in the house to repair the damage to the walls as they had begun to decay. Have you ever heard the saying, 'You shouldn't judge a book by its cover?'"

Several attendees started chatting about examples that they have had by judging prior to really knowing the facts about a situation.

Priscilla was agreeing with the crowd, but her mind still wasn't fully there. She was now thinking about her own salvation. But was still trying hard not to miss anything the Bishop was teaching.

Bishop continued, "Let's take a look at Luke 6:37 & 38. This scripture sums up the exterior wall for this section on Others. I need a volunteer to read this from the King James Version please."

A volunteer in the front row read aloud.

> 37 **Judge not**, and ye shall not be judged: condemn not, and ye shall not be condemned: forgive, and ye shall be forgiven: 38 Give, and it shall be given unto you; good measure, pressed down, and shaken together, and running over, shall **men** give into your bosom. For with the same measure that ye mete withal it shall be measured to you again.
> Luke 6:37-38 KJV

"Thank you." Bishop stated, "When we see someone on their outside (their exterior walls) we should not assume the things we really don't know. Because we don't want God to condemn us for the things that He knows we have done but forgave us. There are other commands in the scripture but the one that I want everyone in this room to grasp hold of is in verse 38 that tells us to give and MEN will give unto YOU. Most often we read that scripture and assume that it is the Lord blessing us and that is true, but it is given to us through men. That statement alone should open our eyes to the importance of having the best relationship with others."

It was Lisa's turn to interrupt the Bishop as she just blurted out, "I don't get it."

Bishop acknowledged Lisa with a head nod and continued, "God honors the giving of his children. In fact, in Mathew 25 it tells us that whatever we do to the least person it's as if you did it to God. If we treat them badly, God will punish us for it. However, if we treat them well, God will ensure that we are blessed either spiritually or physically."

Lisa stated, "Okay, I believe I get it. But there are so many people out there that will take advantage of those that have a giving heart. I've seen it with my grandmother and it really ticks me off!"

"What a great segue," declared Bishop. "That's why it is so important to be led by the Holy Spirit. There are times when we will be approached by someone that we feel don't deserve it because we are looking at their exterior walls. It's at that point that we must remember that we should look at them through the lens of the Holy Spirit. The Spirit will let us know what to do. Haven't you heard the saying that you may be entertaining an angel unaware. That simply means that you never know who you are really in the room with so we should treat everyone like the Kings and Queens that they are!!! And with that my friends, we are out of time. Please e-mail me any questions that you have at the e-mail address on the handouts that were given to you at the beginning of class."

PART THREE – YOU (the roof)

CHAPTER FIVE

"Of course, it's yours!" exclaimed Priscilla

Steve rebutted, "But we haven't really been together like that in the last few months!"

"Really Steve? You are really going to look in my face and question my loyalty? Well, I guess you do have a point. Ever since we moved out here to the boondocks, we rarely see you. But as we both know it doesn't take a lot. So, what are we going to do?" questioned Priscilla.

"The only option I see for us is to make another trip to the doctor's office. We can barely afford the one that we have," declared Steve.

Priscilla played this conversation in her head repeatedly as she laid on the table trying hard not to focus on the suction sound. The sound was like a loud vacuum cleaner literally sucking the life out of her body. When she was released, Steve was waiting for her in the room with absolutely no expression on his face. Her only response, "It's done."

Three weeks passed and Priscilla remained in a state of unbelief, disappointment, uneasy, and depression all wrapped in one. She wondered if God still loved her after what she had done. So many critics have weighed in on the decisions of expectant mothers. Some say it is the mother's choice while so many others say it's murder. But what concerned her most was, what does Jesus think? At that point, she pulled out her notes from Bishop Justice's class on the J portion of JOY. She found the handout that had the chart that listed the three materials to a solid foundation in Jesus. She read the entire 13th chapter of 1 Corinthians. She read Romans 10:9. Then she reflected on the session on Others at Pride University when so many young adults gave their lives back to Christ.

At that moment, she felt a strong urge to just speak to God. She proclaimed in a demanding audible voice, "Lord, take control of my life. I no longer want to live like someone who doesn't know You or Your power. I want to be more like you. I want to develop a relationship with You that no enemy in Hell can ever change. You said that if I believe in my heart that you are the Son of God and speak it with my mouth, I would be saved. Today I'm asking you to save me Lord."

Priscilla continued weeping uncontrollably.

	House Foundation	Physical Purpose	Spiritual Foundation	Spiritual Purpose
JESUS 1 Corinthians 13:13	PLYWOOD	Establish the frame of the house to make sure the cement doesn't go in areas that you don't want your foundation to be in	HOPE	Attitude and Focus • Salvation • Eternal Life • Light Affliction
	STEEL (Rebar)	Adds additional strength to the foundation and reduces the possibility of cracks and leaks in the future	FAITH	Content • Faith Definition • Mustard Seed • Study
	CONCRETE (Cement)	The most important ingredient in a strong foundation. Most professionals encourage DIYers to be sure that the concrete isn't watered down. It must have the correct mixture of concrete and water	LOVE	Action • Love Definition • Commandments • God Loved the world

After about 5 minutes of river like sobbing, the phone rang. It was Lisa's peppy voice on the other end. "Hi girl, I haven't heard from you in a while. How are you?"

Priscilla tried hard to present a voice that didn't sound sad. Instead she matched the peppy voice with, "I'm fine!"

Lisa responded, "I just found out that Bishop Justice was coming back to the church to do a special session on You. As you know, his sessions always get filled up quick. I heard they are doing pre-registration and only those registered can attend his session. If you are interested, I will register and pay for both of us. Consider this my blessing to you. See I was paying attention to the Others seminar at the university."

Priscilla broke down crying all over again.

"Oh my God, Priscilla, what is wrong?" questioned Lisa "What did I say?........ Hello ..... Can you hear me?"

Priscilla couldn't stop crying long enough to get any words out.

Lisa stated emphatically, "I'm hanging up the phone and I'm on my way to your house!"

Ten minutes passed and Lisa was banging on Priscilla's door while yelling, "Open this door girl!"

As she opened the door, Priscilla stated, "You didn't have to come all the way over here. I'm fine." While she was wiping her eyes.

"You scared me, when all I could hear was crying and you wouldn't respond to my questions," declared Lisa.

Priscilla explained, "I know. I just couldn't speak at the moment. I was just so thankful and surprised at how God moves. Before the phone rang, I had a sincere conversation with the Lord. I asked Him to come into my heart like never before. I felt a connection with the Lord and then for you to call and tell me that you were going to bless me with the ability to hear Bishop Justice again. I was just so overwhelmed. You are truly a God sent friend and I love you dearly. Thank you!"

It was Lisa's turn to start bawling like a newborn baby. Priscilla hugged her and the two of them sobbed for about 15 minutes.

They pulled themselves together and discussed the upcoming session with Bishop Justice. They agreed to ride together to ensure that they both attended.

Two weeks passed.

Lisa was again at Priscilla's door yelling, "It's time to ride. We don't want to be late for the Bishop!"

Priscilla ran out the door with bible in hand yelling back, "Let's do this!!"

As the ladies entered the room, Bishop Justice immediately recognized them and said, "Hi ladies, I was looking forward to seeing you two today." He then turned directly to Priscilla and proclaimed how proud he was of her.

With a face of confusion and shock. Priscilla uttered, "Proud of me? Why?"

The room was beginning to fill with an expecting audience so Bishop responded in haste, "Please get with me after today's session." And he hurried to the front of the room.

Five minutes passed then Bishop opened in his signature voice, "JOY!"

He continued, "Today's session is all about You. Yes, You!!! The final letter in leading with JOY."

After a brief recap of the letter J (Jesus) and the letter O (Others). Bishop put up a familiar picture. The picture that Priscilla referred to as the upside-down table.

"This picture represents a house without a roof or the Y that is missing in JOY……YOU!!!" declared Bishop. "I want you all to think about the questions displayed on the white board.

> 1. Is it possible to have a livable structure without a roof?
>
> 2. What happens if there is bad weather (rain, sleet, snow) if there is no roof?
>
> 3. What happens in good weather, when the sun is beaming down, and there is no roof?

He paused for a few minutes, then proceeded. "Just think about the importance of a roof for another minute."

Bishop continued, "It is almost impossible to say you have a physical structure without having and taking care of the roof on top. The same is with JOY. It is virtually impossible to lead with JOY if you never consider and take care of yourself. In fact, the primary cause of roof problems is poor maintenance. And yes, the same is true with You. If you don't properly take care of yourself, it would be extremely difficult to have JOY. Most roofing experts explain that there are three primary things that must be done in order to maintain a roof."

"The first," Bishop held up one finger, "is to remove loose debris. The second" He then puts up a second finger. "is to remove the moss. And finally…." He opened up his arms and drops his shoulders as if to show this should go without saying. "It is imperative to have general inspections and repairs."

"Do you notice something different about Bishop?" Priscilla asked Lisa.

Lisa responded, "I was just about to ask you the same thing. He appears to be off a little. I wonder what's going on with him."

"Yeah, he seems like he is really trying hard to be his normal bubbly vibrant self. He mentioned that he wanted to talk to me after the session. I'll find out what's going on then," replied Priscilla

Bishop asked the ladies to come to the front of the room. They looked at each other like two preschoolers, as if to say they weren't doing anything wrong. As they walked to the front of the room, Bishop declared, "You are not in any trouble. I want to use you two for the illustration."

The ladies sighed in relief.

He asked Priscilla to hold a big tree branch and he put a sombrero on her head full of leaves. "Do you mind getting a little wet?" he whispered in her ear.

She responded, "No not really. But this branch is really heavy!"

Lisa chimed in and said, "You can handle it girl!"

Bishop then asked the girls to race to the back of the room and the one who gets back first will win a prize.

Priscilla spoke up, "Wait she doesn't have a branch or a big hat on her head!"

"On your mark, get set……GO!" yelled Bishop.

Lisa took off. Priscilla was trying to balance the hat so she wouldn't spill the water that Bishop had poured on the leaves. As soon as she got her balance, she started to take a step and the limb moved to the right, the hat tipped to the left and the water and leaves fell to the floor.

The entire audience laughed hysterically.

Bishop chuckled and said, "Let's give Ms. Priscilla a big hand for being such a good sport."

Everyone continued to laugh while they applauded Priscilla for participating in the illustration.

"That's a wonderful illustration of the need to remove loose debris on a roof. Debris can come from limbs weighing on the roof like the branch that Priscilla was holding. Even though she didn't make a step, she wouldn't have been able to run her fastest because of the weight of the limb. I also want to bring to your attention the water that somewhat ruined her clothes. Leaves are another type of debris that clog gutters that doesn't allow the water to run properly away from the roof. But there were a few other things that occurred during this illustration that most people miss. The first was Priscilla's friend encouraging her that she could do this." Bishop paused placing his finger on his forehead with his infamous thought-provoking stance.

He asked the audience, "What do you think about Priscilla's friend encouraging her to do something that I'm sure she has never seen her do before?"

A few hands went up. An older lady in the back responded, "She had confidence that her friend could do all things through Christ who strengthens her. Right?"

Bishop continued standing with the same stance.

A gentleman in the front blurted out, "I believe she just wanted to see her friend make a fool of herself."

 Bishop chuckled again, while the audience laughed out loud.

Priscilla raised her hand and asked, "But she really didn't know what you were going to ask me to do, so technically she shouldn't have encouraged me unless the Holy Spirit was leading her to do so."

"Ah Ha!" Bishop declared. "You are on to something."

He continued, "In the spiritual realm there are many types of debris or weights that keep us from doing what we are called to do. It is important to first know what you are supposed to be doing for the Kingdom so that you aren't persuaded by others to do something that you were NEVER called to do. In this illustration Priscilla wasn't built to hold a huge limb and run a race with a hat full of leaves and water. But because I asked her and her friend encouraged her, she was willing to give it a try. HUGE MISTAKE!!! We see this in our churches and in the workplace, all the time. If you want to have JOY, you must determine what your true calling is so that you don't take on excess debris. There are several tests or questionnaires that will show you what your spiritual gifts are. I encourage you to pick up the handout that list a few of the online questionnaires before you leave today."

Priscilla whispered to Lisa, "I forgive you my friend." And they both laughed.

Bishop then stated, "Another point I want to make is to be sure you know who your friends really are. I'm sure you all remember the story of Job and how his friends treated him as he was going through. In chapters 4 – 25, Job's friends provided long speeches about why God allows men to suffer. Most of which was inaccurate, purely their opinion. Now compare that to the friends of the paralyzed man in Mark 2:1-5. In verse 5, we learn that it was because of the faith of the friends that Jesus healed the paralyzed man. I don't know about you, but those are the type of friends I need around me!"

Lisa had this weird look on her face. She wondered if Bishop was insinuating that she was a bad friend for Priscilla. Just as Priscilla looked over at Lisa, Bishop addressed the concern look. "Please don't think I am stating that the ladies that helped with the illustration are not good friends, I'm simply showing the importance of knowing who you keep company with."

Both ladies smiled at one another in agreement with the clarification provided.

Bishop continued, "The final point I want to make regarding debris, is that a well-constructed roof is made to handle a certain amount of debris. In fact, it wouldn't be a roof if it couldn't handle majority of the rain, leaves, limbs, snow, hail, and sun rays. I believe if the roof could talk, it would take pride in the fact that it prevents major damage to the structure and the foundation. You wouldn't hear the roof complain about another storm or another hot summer day. No sir, that roof knows exactly what it was built to do. The same is with us. Can I get a volunteer to read James 1:2-4?"

One of the gentlemen in front stood up and read:

> "2Consider it pure joy, my brothers and sisters, whenever you face trials of many kinds, 3because you know that the testing of your faith produces perseverance. 4 Let

perseverance finish its work so that you may
be mature and complete, not lacking
anything."
James 1:2-4 NIV

"Thank you, sir." Bishop expressed "When most people experience an uncomfortable time in their lives, their first inclination is to pray that God remove the trial quickly. Just the other day, I stumped my toe on the end of the bed and I prayed that God would remove the pain right then. I didn't want to wait the few minutes that it normally takes for the pain to subside. I mean it really hurt! I'm sure God was thinking, REALLY, you called on me for a stumped toe."

The audience laughed.

He continued, "My friends, we must take heed to the instruction of James. Whatever we are going through we must count it Joy, having the faith to believe that it is working together to mature us in our Christian walk and ultimately increasing our wisdom."

Bishop spoke the last few words as if he had a tickle in his throat. After he forced the word wisdom out of his mouth, he had a coughing fit.

One of the ladies in the front gave him a bottle of water. When he composed himself, he informed the audience that this was a good time to take a 15-minute break.

CHAPTER SIX

Fifteen minutes went by, 20, 22…. At the 25-minute mark the audience began discussing what could be delaying him. It was 30 minutes before Bishop would return to the room. He attempted to muster up the energy to provide the booming voice to say JOY in his normal fashion. To those who have been to his sessions before, they knew it wasn't the same.

Bishop mustered up a huge smile and apologetically announced, "The session must go on! Please forgive the delay. The information that I must share this afternoon is necessary. So again, the session must go on! We left off talking about counting it all JOY during trials and the removal of debris from our lives. The next important roof maintenance is the removal of moss."

Lisa turned to Priscilla and asked, "What in the world is moss?"

"Girl I use to think it was a nice pretty green carpet that my parents had on top of their house, until my dad informed me that it was not a good thing to have it on your roof," responded Priscilla.

Bishop then displayed a picture of a roof with moss on it.

"Take a look at the picture displayed on the screen. Look at it from the right to the left to see how the roof starts with a little dirt then some moss spots begin to appear. Finally, the roof is covered with moss that resembles green carpet. Some roofers describe moss as a slow kill because it seems harmless at first but if left untreated it causes so much damage that the entire roof must be replaced. This moss is like having a prideful heart. I personally love how the Message bible describes Pride in Proverbs 16:18, 19. Please read this aloud from my bible." Bishop handed his bible to Priscilla to read.

> 18 First pride, then the crash—the bigger the ego, the harder the fall. 19 It's better to live humbly among the poor than to live it up among the rich and famous.
> Proverbs 16:18,19 Message Bible

He continued, "Thank you. Just like the dirt on the roof that eventually turns into yucky moss, pride has the tendency to inch up on Christians. First you have a little confidence that turns into pride. I personally like to call it self-reliance instead of God reliance. But it ALWAYS ends up in a fall. I have a good friend who became a pastor of a church the same year that I did … just a few…maybe several years ago." He said with a smile on his face. "Anyway, my friend had a gift of bringing souls to Christ and his church grew quickly. He was a phenomenal preacher. I had the great opportunity to visit his church about 5 years after he started. The message was unsettling. His message was more about what he had done for the members and how they needed to bless him as their shepherd and less about God or scripture. At the time, I dismissed it because all congregations need a little reprimand every once in a while. However, when I went back the next year, the message was very similar. I looked around and the congregation was significantly smaller than it was. As I walked to my car in the parking lot, I overheard a few of his members comment on how they were tired of every service being about him and his family or about money. They continued to say how much he had changed, and they didn't believe he was aware of the change. I proceeded to my car and prayed all the way home about how to approach my friend. As I entered my house, I heard the phone ring. Guess who it was?"

Priscilla spoke up, "It was your friend!"

Bishop smiled in agreement, "That's right. He was calling to ask me what I thought about the service and wanted to get my feedback on why so many of his members have left the church. I thought to myself, WOW God really moved quickly. I used the sandwich method of providing feedback. I first told him how awesome his messages are and how I always loved his dissection of the Word referencing Hebrew and Greek. I then shared with him the concern about focusing more on himself instead of the needs of the congregation. Reality is no one wants to hear how good your life is ALL the time when they are going through major situations in their life. Then I wrapped up the feedback sandwich with, the good news that he has several faithful members who would support him if he acknowledges his area of weakness and they would encourage others to come back to the church. But it must start with him."

This time Lisa spoke up, "What did he do?"

"I could tell during the conversation, he was somewhat hesitant to receive what I was telling him, but we had been friends for a long time. Ultimately, he heeded the advice and he now have thousands of faithful members across three states." He responded

Several people in the audience said, "WOW!"

Bishop continued, "Yes, it is amazing. I'm just thankful that he had/has a strong foundation and we were able to refer to scriptures like 1 Peter 5:5 where it encourages us to clothe ourselves in humility. Also, we discussed Isaiah 2:12 and 23:9 that explains the Lord would bring down the proud and lofty. We concluded with a discussion on not being wise in our own opinions (Jeremiah 9:23 & Proverbs 3:7) nor rely on our own strength and understanding (Proverbs 3:5). This situation actually carries us to the last important piece of roof maintenance – General Inspection & Repair."

Priscilla asked Lisa, "Is it me or does Bishop appear to be rushing through this session?"

Lisa nodded her head in agreement, "Yeah, I don't think he is feeling well."

"I hope he will be alright. Maybe we will still chat after we finish today; I will ask him then." Priscilla stated.

Bishop grabbed his bottle of water as he ended yet another coughing spell. He then popped what looked like a cough drop in his mouth, apologized, and continued the presentation. "Checking a roof consistently prevents costly repairs from occurring. The same is with our spiritual walk. It is imperative that we have a trusted accountability partner in the ministry to prevent the wrath of God. Scripture tells us that it is difficult for us to see our own problems. We usually can't tell that we are headed down the wrong path until it becomes extremely bad. But if we have at least one person that we trust to tell us the honest truth in love it can decrease the amount of turmoil that we bring on ourselves. Just like the example that I used with my friend. He was headed down a path that would have prevented thousands of souls from being saved (at least under his watch). But because we were able to go to the Word, pray for one another in intercession, we have helped each other over the years."

Wiping sweat from his brow, Bishop explained, "I apologize everyone, we are going to have to end this session a little early today. I have a handout with the details regarding the YOU section of JOY. I sincerely apologize, but I'm not feeling my best. Please pray my strength and I will see you next time."

A couple of the attendees spoke out. One said, "We hope you feel better." Another shouted, "Thanks for the information."

Priscilla walked up to Bishop and before she could say anything he stated, "The Lord showed me that you are ready to be used for His Kingdom work. This came at a time when I had been praying about someone that could help me as the demand for JOY seminars are consistently increasing. Unfortunately, I'm unable to go into details currently. Please write down your full name, address, and phone number. I will be in touch with you in a few days."

She wrote her contact information in big print and below it she wrote…… ***We are praying for you!!***

On the way home, Priscilla and Lisa had a great conversation about the entire JOY concept. They talked about how it seemed so obvious. Jesus first, then others, and making sure You position yourself to receive the blessings that God has for you. Both ladies agreed to be each other's accountability partner. They agreed to intercede for each other as the Lord laid it on their hearts. They also agreed to be honest in love when they saw the other succumb to a fault. And finally, they agreed to be the ear that they need when they just need to talk with no judgement.

Before Priscilla got out of the car she turned to her sister with all sincerity in her eyes and in her heart uttered, "I LOVE YOU!!!"

Lisa's eyes swelled as she responded, "I LOVE YOU TOO, MY SISTA!!!"

PART FOUR – JOY Established (the house)

CHAPTER SEVEN

It was a typical Saturday morning of listening to Gospel music and cleaning the house from top to bottom. Or was it? Normally, Priscilla would bellow out Kirk Franklin and Yolanda Adams songs as if she was on stage at a sold-out concert. However, this Saturday she was singing hymns that she witnessed her grandmothers singing as they were cleaning. It was when she attempted to harmonize how she knew "it was the blood" when emotions began to flood her like the blood of Jesus was actually flowing from His body onto hers. She fell to her knees and asked the Lord to tell her what it was that He wanted her to do. There was silence. She stretched out, prostrate on her floor pleading to the physically invisible higher power to show her exactly what her next steps were to be. She laid there for what seemed like half a day, but in reality, it was about 45 minutes when she heard the phone ring. Not wanting to lose the connection she had with the Spirit, she continued to lay face down. Continuing to plead her case she began to speak aloud.

"Oh Lord, please hear my prayer. I'm asking you to show me without a shadow of doubt my next move. I need to know with the upmost certainty that it is you guiding my footsteps. I need to know that it is not my will, but it is Your will. I realize that you give us free will and you expect us to study your word and align our actions with those of Your son Jesus. But Lord, at this moment I need a little more. I need for you to make it crystal clear. I don't trust myself. I've made several moves that most people would say were wrong. I also know that all things are working for my good. But again Lord, I don't want to make the same types of mistakes over and over again. I need to know that You are guiding my footsteps. I need to know without a shadow of doubt that it is You that I'm listening to. Lord, please just make it clear."

The phone rings again.

Priscilla continued with her petition. "Lord, I need you to make it clear."

The phone continues to ring. It appears that the caller is determined to get an answer.

Reluctantly, Priscilla rises from the floor and walks over to the phone. Just as she reaches to pick up the phone, it stops ringing. She heads back to the area in her floor where she could continue pleading her case. As she drops on one knee the phone rings again.

"Ugh" Priscilla shouted in anguish. "They better not hang up this time."

She walks over to the phone and shouts, "HELLO!"

"Hello, is this Priscilla?" the caller inquired.

Priscilla responded, "May I ask who is calling?"

"This is Bishop Justice from the JOY seminars," The caller answered.

"Oh Bishop, how are you? Please forgive my tone I was in the middle of something," Priscilla declared.

Bishop then stated, "Please forgive my interruption, I've been trying to call you all morning. I will not take up much of your time. I was wondering if you were busy this weekend. I will be at a local church conducting a four-hour seminar covering all three portions of JOY. My hope is that you would be able to attend and assist with the seminar."

There was complete silence for about 30 seconds, then Bishop questioned, "Priscilla are you still there?"

Priscilla shouted, "Oh my God, You are so Amazing. You are an Awesome God!!! Glory!!! Hallelujah!!! Glory!!! Thank you!!!"

Bishop then responded, "Ummm, Yes, God is Awesome, Yes He is Amazing, I praise Him with you my sister!"

"I'm so sorry Bishop. I was just praying for direction and your phone call was so timely." Priscilla stated "But yes! I am available this weekend and I would be honored to assist you with the seminar."

The two discussed the details of Priscilla's responsibilities and agreed to meet an hour before the start of the seminar.

Upon hanging up the phone. Priscilla went right back into praise. She thanked God for hearing her prayer and for making her next move crystal clear. She jumped, she yelled, she cried, she laughed, she ran, she bowed, she jumped and ran some more, until she was literally wet from perspiration.

Falling back down to her knees, she verbalized her appreciation. "THANK YOU THANK YOU THANK YOU!!!"

The rest of the week flew by.

Priscilla rose early on Saturday morning to ensure that she was at the church at least 30 minutes prior to the agreed meeting time. She drove into the parking lot at the same time as a big black truck. Bishop Justice got out of the passenger side of the vehicle extremely slow. He greeted Priscilla and introduced her to his daughter who was driving the truck.

Bishop continued, "I'm so glad you could make it. Are you ready?"

"Absolutely, I've been in prayer since we spoke!" Priscilla responded.

They placed all the seminar materials on a hand truck and walked into the building to set up.

Bishop turned to Priscilla, "As we discussed, I will cover the J, you will do the Others section, then I will close the session out with the Y. The Lord already showed me that you are ready. Just relax and allow the Lord to speak through you. Feel free to share your personal examples of interactions with Others. The audience can easily make the connection when we share personal experiences. But again, relax and let Jesus take control."

Priscilla was so excited and truly honored that Bishop asked her to help him with the seminar and so thankful that the Lord saw enough in her to give her this opportunity. Although she was super excited, she couldn't help but think about how Bishop's appearance was drastically different from the last time that she saw him. She said a little prayer for him in her head, then quickly reviewed her notes for the section on Others.

Bishop declared, "It's show time. Priscilla let's make sure the guest of honor is in the place." He stuck out his hand.

Priscilla showed a confused look but put her hand out to grab his. Squeezing her hand, they began to pray.

"Oh Lord, our honored companion, without you we can do nothing. We ask that you have your way in this place today. If there is a soul that needs to be saved, help us in guiding them through the plan of salvation. If there is a hurting soul or a backslider, help us in steering them back on the straight and narrow. If there is anyone that is sick in their bodies, help us to let them know that by Your stripes they are healed. Now Lord we know what our assignment is in the natural, but we come on an assignment as willing vessels to be used for the Glory of

Your Kingdom. So, if we don't get through the information that we have prepared, that's okay. Because we know that our plans are not your plans. Our mission is to spread JOY. We pray earnestly that every soul that leaves here today leaves with TRUE JOY that could never be shaken by the snares of anyone not like you. We give you all the Honor and all the Glory. For it is in Jesus matchless name we pray. AMEN!!!"

Priscilla said, "AMEN!!! What an amazing prayer!"

As attendees began filling the room, Priscilla noticed the various age groups and backgrounds of the attendees. Although the session was at a Baptist church, the attendees were from various religions and all races. It was as if she was getting a glimpse of what heaven would be like.

When the clock struck 10:00, Bishop greeted the crowd in his normal fashion, "JOY!"

He continued with his opening illustration and request to have the attendees describe what they saw.

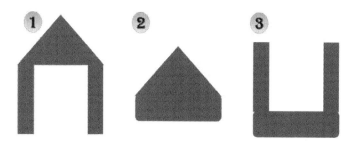

Priscilla looked around the room. She witnessed the same facial expressions that she and her friend Lisa had on their faces when they were first introduced to JOY. She giggled inside realizing that soon they would be enlightened about each of the three shapes and how it will all come together by the end of the conference.

Bishop went through his normal process of asking attendees to describe what they saw and after 2 minutes he stated, "if we were to combine all three pictures with what is missing in each it would be a house full of JOY. Our objective for today's conference is to know what true JOY looks like." He then pulled up the completed picture.

He continued, "The reason why we did this exercise in viewing the shapes was to see how easy it is to be perceived as being whole, being healed, being happy, being complete when we don't have something to compare or contrast. Now that you see the complete house, it is easy to identify the missing pieces of the previous pictures."

Bishop paused for a second realizing he hadn't introduced his partner. He motioned for Priscilla to come to the center of the room where he was standing. "It is my esteemed pleasure to introduce you to my co-facilitator. This is the first time that I'm presenting with a partner. I'm super excited about the passion that she brings. Ms. Priscilla is a recent graduate from Grace University where she majored in Business specifically in Leadership. She will present the second portion of today's seminar on the letter O. I know you all will be just as thrilled as I am to have her join us today."

"Oh my God!" Priscilla said under her breathe. She thought to herself, "I wish he hadn't said all of that. What if I don't live up to the expectations of the attendees. What if I can't remember what I'm supposed to say or do. What if I didn't hear the Lord right and I'm really not supposed to be doing this. What if I make a mockery of God. What if…… What if….. What if….."

In the middle of all of Priscilla's what ifs, Bishop walks over and whispered in her ear, "God's got you!"

At that moment, a peace came over Priscilla as if it were God himself speaking directly into her ear. She then remembered her encounter with the Lord earlier that week. She knew she had to focus on what God had called her to do so she began praying and quoting scriptures in her mind. "He will never leave me nor forsake me.......The footsteps of a good man are ordered by the Lord......I can do all things through Christ that strengthens me!" She was going on and on until she realized that there were very few people in the room. An entire hour had gone by and she didn't realize that Bishop was just about finished with the letter J and the attendees were taking a break.

Bishop walked over to Priscilla and stated, "When they come back from their break, we are going to head right into the letter O."

She responded "Okay." She moved to the whiteboard and wrote the same three questions that Bishop asked the attendees to answer when she was present for His session on the letter O.

1. Do you LOVE Everyone?

2. What type of people are easy to LOVE?

3. What type of people are more difficult to LOVE?

As the attendees entered the room, Priscilla looked each of them in the eye. She felt the intense desire to be an effective leader coupled with the need to have JOY in every person that entered the room. She glanced over at Bishop to see if he felt the same energy from them. He gave her a proud fatherly smile as if to say, "Yes, that's why you were chosen!"

The feeling she had at that moment was so intense primarily because she knew without a doubt that she was about to do what God wanted her to do at that moment. She said to herself, "Wow, what a feeling. Thank you, Jesus!" She moved to the center of the room and bellowed out as loud as she could "JOY!"

CHAPTER EIGHT

Four weeks after Priscilla co-facilitated the seminar with Bishop Justice, she was lugging in 6 heavy bags of groceries into the house when she heard her telephone ringing. She dropped the bags near the front door, ran to pick up the phone just as it stopped ringing. "Oh well," she thought, "they will call back." She ran back out to the car to get her baby girl and brought her into the house. The phone rang again.

Priscilla answered. "Hello."

The voice on the other end asked, "Is this Priscilla?"

She responded, "May I ask who is calling?"

The voice responded, "I'm calling from Bush Financial Services and I was wondering if you would be available for an interview on Wednesday at 9:00am? I noticed that your current address is in Pittsboro. This position is in Midland. Are you interested in relocating to Midland?"

Priscilla quickly responded, "Yes ma'am I am interested in relocating and will be at the interview on Wednesday at 9:00am."

After the caller gave Priscilla the specific details, she hung up the phone and ran around the room thanking God. She completely forgot that she applied for the entry level position back in her hometown. In the most humble and thankful fashion she praised God for working things out in a way that she never anticipated. She cried so hard that it forced her daughter to cry as well. Naturally the baby didn't realize her mom's tears were tears of JOY!!!

The next week she received a call from Bush Financial Services extending an offer of full-time employment with an excellent salary and of course benefits. She accepted and immediately planned to move 4 hours back to her hometown.

The first thing that she needed to do was call Steve and let him know that she was moving. The relationship had really become somewhat estranged since the last pregnancy. He spent most of his time at work or with other women. Just depended on who you asked. Steve would say he was at work while Priscilla's girls would say he was at the club dancing with other women. Nonetheless, Priscilla thought the right thing to do would be to tell him they were leaving.

She called his phone several times that morning with no answer. It was very frustrating since he said he was off that day. She tried calling one more time and her suspicions became a reality.

Another woman answered the phone with a rather happy kind of excited voice. "Helloooo"

Priscilla said, "Hello, who is this?"

Then she heard Steve in the background say, "You don't answer my phone!" and hangs up the phone.

Of course, Priscilla is furious. She packs up the baby's bag and headed out the door. Just as she was backing out of the driveway, her friend Lisa pulls in behind her.

Lisa gets out the car and with tears in her eyes asks Priscilla if she had heard.

Priscilla is fuming but she managed to get the words out in a hateful tone, "Heard what?"

Lisa responded, "It's Bishop Justice."

Feeling agitated Priscilla pops her lips, raises one eyebrow, exhales and questioned, "What about Bishop?"

"He died." Lisa cried out.

Priscilla froze.

She didn't know what to say or how to feel. All she could muster up was "What?....What do you mean? I was just with him a few weeks ago."

Lisa unhooked the baby and took her out of the car seat then said, "Let's go inside and I will tell you what I know."

Priscilla followed Lisa into the house. She was still somewhat numb by the news of Bishop and still very upset that another woman had just answered Steve's phone.

"I know you were headed somewhere, but I figured you would want to know about Bishop." Lisa explained. "I was at a church meeting this morning and one of the mothers of the church informed us that Bishop had cancer in the throat. He was diagnosed at stage 4 not long after he presented on the letter J where we first met."

Priscilla nodded her head.

Lisa continued, "Well he took a turn for the worse two weeks ago and just never recovered." She paused. "What else is going on Priscilla?"

At that moment Priscilla broke down. She yelled, "Just when I thought everything was working in my favor. Everything falls apart. God what is going on?"

Just as she began to cry, Lisa grabbed her and said, "everything is working in your favor. It may not seem like it right now but trust me the best is yet to come."

Priscilla pulled herself together and shared with Lisa what had just happened with Steve. Then Lisa said something that completely caught Priscilla off guard.

"Oh, HELL No!!! Let's go ride up on that ......" Lisa shouted before she caught herself and lowered her tone of voice. "I mean that is really messed up. Let's go and have a conversation with him."

"That's exactly what I had planned to do before you blocked me in." Priscilla responded "However, now that I have had a moment to think. That's just what the enemy wants me to do...go back to a place that isn't becoming of where I'm headed. You know I just received a job offer and I will be moving back to my hometown."

Lisa screamed, "NO...don't leave me!!"

"I have to do what's best for me and my child." Priscilla said

Lisa agreed, "I know. Do you want to go to Bishop's funeral? It is going to be in a couple of days in his hometown about 2 hours away."

Priscilla responded, "Sure. We can ride together. Thank you, Lisa, for being such a great friend. I truly appreciate you coming. This was an ordained visit. But there is something that I must take care of right now. I'll meet you at your house to go to the funeral."

"Please don't do anything that you will regret later. Pray before you take any type of action. Love you girl." Lisa declared. Then she drove off.

Just as Priscilla was getting the baby ready to head out the house, in walks Steve begging, "Before you go off on me, please let me explain."

Priscilla stood firmly, tilted her head to the side and simply said, "Explain."

He proceeded, "She came over to help me study for an upcoming Economics exam."

Priscilla started laughing uncontrollably.

Steve asked, "Why are you laughing?"

"Because you are a joke." Priscilla declared. "The reason why I was calling you was to let you know that I will be moving back to Midland next week. I received a great job opportunity."

"What about me? You can't take my child four hours away!" professed Steve.

Priscilla laughed again. "Yes, I can, and I will. You should be glad. This way you don't have to try so hard to hide the fact that you want to see other people. As a matter of fact, now may be a good time for us to officially say that we are going to see other people."

Steve was somewhat caught off guard. Although this is what he wanted, he wanted to be the one to officially call it off. The only thing he could think to say was, "Just remember that this is my child too."

Priscilla smirked and responded, "Yeah, I know. Bless our hearts! Have a great evening. Good bye!"

Steve kissed his daughter and walked out the door.

Priscilla looked in the mirror on the wall in amazement. She couldn't believe how strong she was during the conversation with Steve.

Several days past and Steve hadn't contacted Priscilla at all. In fact, Priscilla was wondering if he was going to come by prior to them moving back to Midland. The move was only 2 days away.

She got dressed and drove to Lisa's house. On the ride to Bishop's funeral, they discussed what occurred with Steve. Lisa expressed how proud she was of Priscilla and let her know that amazing things would happen soon. She encouraged her to think positive and remember everything that she had learned at the JOY seminars.

The funeral lasted almost 5 hours. There were so many people sharing their stories about Bishop and how he impacted their lives. As they were leaving a middle-aged woman tapped Priscilla on the shoulder. It was Bishop's daughter. Priscilla immediately recognized her from when she drove Bishop to the seminar that she co-facilitated.

"Thank you so much for coming Priscilla." Bishop's daughter said. "Do you still live at the Pittsboro address you gave to my dad?"

Looking surprised, Priscilla stated "Yes, why?"

Bishop's daughter responded, "We sent a package to you. Everything is explained in the letter. Thanks again for coming." She hugged Priscilla then walked off.

As they drove back to Pittsboro, Lisa asked "What was that all about?"

Priscilla stated, "His daughter said that they sent me a package and that there would be a letter explaining the contents. I hope I get it before I move. Speaking of the move, I've got a lot of packing to do. My mom will be here with the U-Haul early in the morning. I'm réally going to miss you!"

"I'm going to miss you as well. But we will stay in touch. Let me know when you guys get to Midland. Love you!" stated Lisa.

"Love you back!" declared Priscilla.

Lisa got out of the car and Priscilla drove home to pack up her belongings.

Early the next morning, Priscilla heard a huge truck pull into the driveway. She immediately thought it was her mom. When she opened the door, she realized it was a delivery man asking if she was Priscilla. The man asked her to sign a piece of paper acknowledging receipt of the package then began unloading several boxes. After he placed the last box in her front room, he handed her an envelope then left.

The letter read:

> Dear Priscilla,
>
> When you receive this letter, my spirit will be in the bosom of the Lord. I wanted you to know that I'm so thankful for meeting you. You have a sincere spirit that is like no one that I have met. Many people will not understand you and that's okay. God knows

that you have a genuine heart, so He has blessed you with a gift that allows you to discern things. Don't take this gift lightly. Always know that it was given to you to be used for the building of His Kingdom and not for your glory. Use it to uplift and not tear down.

The boxes that have been delivered contain all my material that I've used to conduct the JOY seminars. Please do not allow the "JOY" vision to die with my physical body. The mantle is being passed on to you. Also in this envelope is the contact information for individuals and organizations that have asked me to come present JOY leadership. Reach out to them as soon as possible to let them know that you are continuing with the seminars.

Please do not allow anyone to steal the JOY that you have received from God.

Sincerely, Bishop Justice

She had finally received what she had been praying for…… A JOB and something she didn't realize she needed…..true **JOY!!!**

■■■ ■

TO BE CONTINUED.....

JOY Leadership Charts

JESUS 1 Corinthians 13:13	House Foundation	Physical Purpose	Spiritual Foundation	Spiritual Purpose
	PLYWOOD	Establish the frame of the house to make sure the cement doesn't go in areas that you don't want your foundation to be in	HOPE	Attitude and Focus • Salvation • Eternal Life • Light Affliction
	STEEL (Rebar)	Adds additional strength to the foundation and reduces the possibility of cracks and leaks in the future	FAITH	Content • Faith Definition • Mustard Seed • Study
	CONCRETE (Cement)	The most important ingredient in a strong foundation. Most professionals encourage DIYers to be sure that the concrete isn't watered down it must have the correct mixture of concrete and water	LOVE	Action • Love Definition • Commandments • God Loved the world

OTHERS 1 Corinthians 3:10-14	House Structure	Physical Purpose	Spiritual Structure	Spiritual Purpose
	JOISTS (Floor and Ceiling)	Floor Joists – important to the stability and security of the floor. Installed in the early stages of the flooring. Ceiling Joists - to tie the rooms/walls together making a box and to lay a foundation for the ceiling	LOVE John 15:10 - 15	Stability • Complete Joy Security • Commandment to love others = friends of God Sacrifice • Lay down life
	WALLS (Load Bearing & Exterior)	Load Bearing Walls – holds up the intersection of joists that create the flooring, usually of an upper room floor. Exterior Walls – The beautification walls. The walls that most people can see.	HOLY SPIRIT Romans 8:26 Galatians 5:25 1 Corinthians 2:13 Luke 6:37, 38	Guidance • Strength • Wisdom • Judgement

YOU James 1:2-4	Roof Maintenance	Physical Purpose	Spiritual Maintenance	Spiritual Purpose
	Remove loose DEBRI	Debris can come from limbs weighing on the roof which could cause the roof to cave. Or from leaves and dirt in the gutters which can cause water damage.	ELIMINATE EXCESS WEIGHT	Weight • Non-Friends • Busy Work (Not walking in calling) • Complaining
	Remove MOSS	Roof is the ideal place for moss to grow. It seems harmless at first but will cause irreparable damage if left untreated.	ELIMINATE PRIDE	Relying on Self • Understanding • Opinions • Strength
	General Inspection & Repair	Checking a roof frequently prevents costly repairs from occurring.	SPIRITUAL COVERING	Accountability • Prayer Partner • Intercessor • Advisor

Case for the Book

For someone who has led many people, groups, organizations, etc. successfully....

- "All leaders should read this book because it helps one to identify what areas in their life and profession need improvement. It encourages one to be honest with self and God. Self-awareness is key in leadership. Leaders who understand their own emotions, personality and strengths/weaknesses can better serve and engage others."
- "This book may be exactly what a seasoned leader needs to encourage them to keep up the hard work and that there is always someone out there benefitting from them."
- "Every leader, at times, need to assess where they are; positive/negative effects of their leadership. This book will allow them the opportunities to examine first their relationship with God. He is the ideal leader. Then examine their relationship/leadership with others."

For someone who hasn't had a formal leadership title.......

- "It encourages and shows everyone how to obtain true JOY. I like that it touches the Christian and those who haven't accepted Christ, yet. After this read, you'll either become a Christian, leading life in JOY or have a stronger relationship with God experiencing more JOY!"

- "This book may be the encouragement someone needs to start their journey of being an inspiration to others."
- "If one desires to be in leadership, this book will offer them a look into leadership......leading involves more than themselves; but Others."

∎∎

Most valuable lessons I've learned as a leader...

When all leaders of any organization are on one accord regarding JOY, it is amazing what happens even during hard times.

It is also strongly encouraged to use this approach in the workplace, civic organizations, sport teams, etc. After all this is not just a book or even a concept...It should be a Lifestyle!!!

Making yourself available for God's use in every situation will yield positive results 100% of the time. There may be times when you will be uncomfortable, vulnerable, and may even seem soft but it IS worth it!!!

∎∎

Contact Information

Website:	www.EstablishingJOY.com
Twitter:	@Nicole_JOYLead
Linkedin:	linkedin.com/in/nicolecrewscarter
Facebook:	facebook.com/Establishing-JOY
E-mail:	EstablishingJOY@gmail.com

NICOLE CARTER, can best be described as a thermostat that changes the climate of any room. Her contagious smile illustrates the vision that God wants for all of His children – true JOY. She was raised in the church and has served as Sunday School secretary, teacher and superintendent. Nicole also assisted as an usher, choir director, media, finance, and pastor's aide committee member. Currently, she faithfully serves God's congregation as a pastor's wife.

She is a middle school CTE teacher with an extensive business, education, and presentation background. She spent 20 years as a leader at a Fortune 200 corporation while teaching as an adjunct professor at local community colleges. She has a Bachelor's degree in Finance from East Carolina University and a MBA from Averett University. She has received several designations through Toastmasters International (a professional speaking organization). Now, having retired from corporate America, she finds joy in developing long lasting relationships with her middle school students, presenting improvement strategies at leadership conferences, and spending time with her family.

Made in the USA
Columbia, SC
10 August 2019